AT THE Aquarium

MARVELOUS MAMMALS

by
Mignonne Gunasekara

BEARPORT PUBLISHING

Minneapolis, Minnesota

PHOTO CREDITS

All images are courtesy of Shutterstock.com, unless otherwise specified. With thanks to Getty Images, Thinkstock Photo and iStockphoto. Plant Vectors Throughout – Baksiabat, MicroOne. Front Cover – Sanjatosic, Willyam Bradberry, Kris Wiktor. 4–5 – In Green. 6–7 – vkilikov, Rich Carey, bernd.neeser, Eduard Radu, The_Pixel, Nadzin. 8–9 – Willyam Bradberry, gilkop. Dray van Beeck, yaichatchai. 10–11 – Chase Dekker, Giuseppe_R, Wanida_Sri. 12–13 – Roman Kharlamov, Mikhail Cheremkin. 14–15 – worldclassphoto, Leonardo Gonzalez, Stacy Funderburke, Claudiovidri. 16–17 – wildestanimal, robert_s, Tory Kallman, Foto 4440. 18–19 – David A. Litman, Mariya Serezhkina, Alex Chernyavsky . 20–21 – polarman, Bernhard Staehli,GTW, mallinka. 22–23 – FloridaStock , Fly_and_Dive, Alexey, Sergey Novikov, Rotanov, JGA, Ann in the uk.

Library of Congress Cataloging-in-Publication Data is available at www.loc.gov or upon request from the publisher.

ISBN: 978-1-64747-406-5 (hardcover)
ISBN: 978-1-64747-413-3 (paperback)
ISBN: 978-1-64747-420-1 (ebook)

For more information, write to Bearport Publishing, 5357 Penn Avenue South, Minneapolis, MN 55419.
Printed in the United States of America.

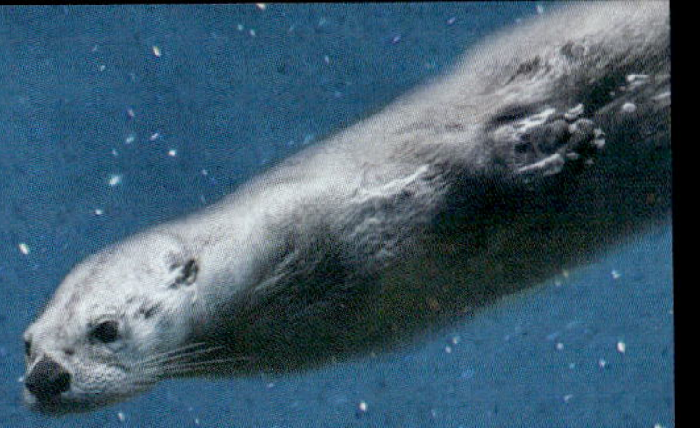

CONTENTS

WELCOME TO THE AQUARIUM!

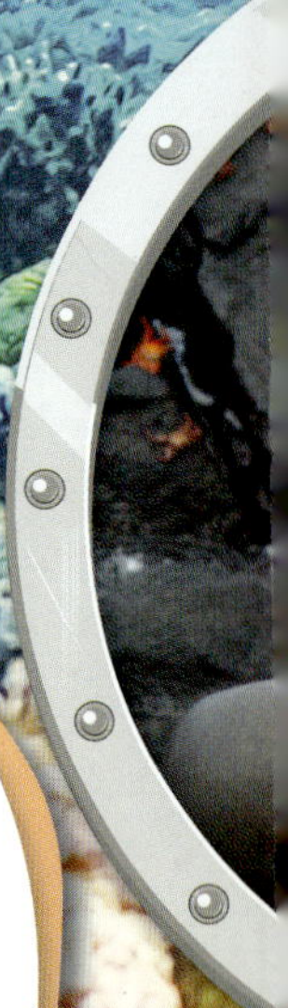

Welcome to the aquarium. Aquariums look after sea animals. Many aquariums do lots of work to protect wild animals, too.

Let's look at eight marvelous sea mammals. Mammals are warm-blooded animals that feed their babies with milk from their own bodies.

Warm-blooded animals can keep their bodies warm whether it's hot or cold outside.

SEA COW

The sea cow is called the lady of the sea in some places.

Sea cows live in warm, **shallow** waters. People who spotted them long ago thought they were **mermaids**.

These animals are so big that most **predators** don't attack them. But young sea cows may be eaten by crocodiles, orcas, and sharks.

Sea cows sometimes get hit by boats or stuck in fishing nets.

Sea cows spend their days eating seagrass.

BOTTLENOSE DOLPHIN

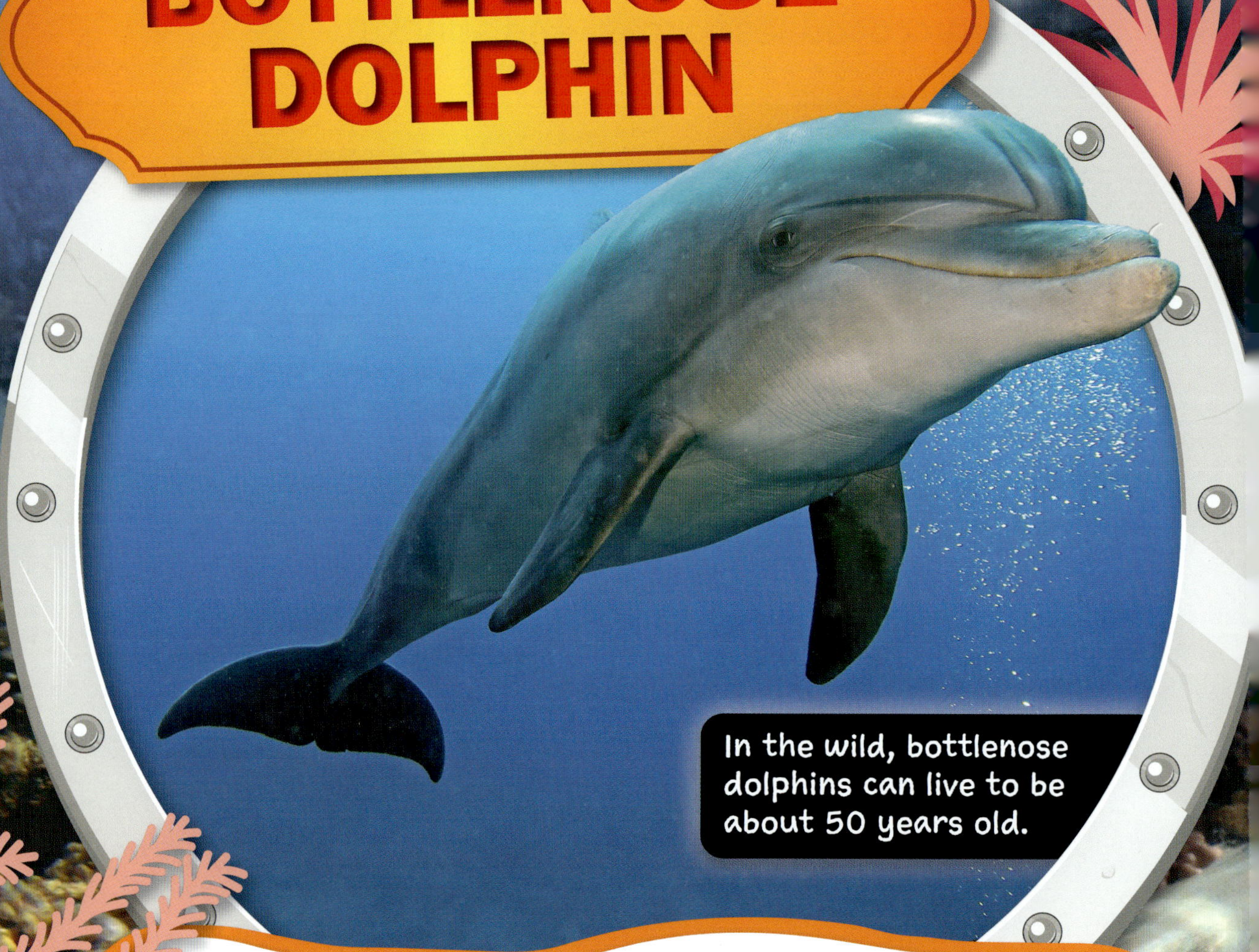

In the wild, bottlenose dolphins can live to be about 50 years old.

Bottlenose dolphins live in warm ocean waters all around the world. They are very smart animals.

Dolphins make clicking sounds that travel through the water. The clicks help dolphins learn where things are and how big they are.

Bottlenose dolphins live and travel in small groups known as **pods**.

Dolphins need to watch out for fishing nets.

SEA OTTER

Sea otters have the thickest fur of any animal!

Sea otters swim and float in the water. They float on their backs while sleeping.

Sea otters eat **prey** such as clams, sea urchins, and crabs.

Sea otters often float with a rock on their chest. They use this rock to smash open the shells of animals they eat.

WALRUS

There are two kinds of walruses—the Atlantic and the Pacific.

Their large size keeps walruses safe from most predators. But they can be hurt or eaten by polar bears and orcas.

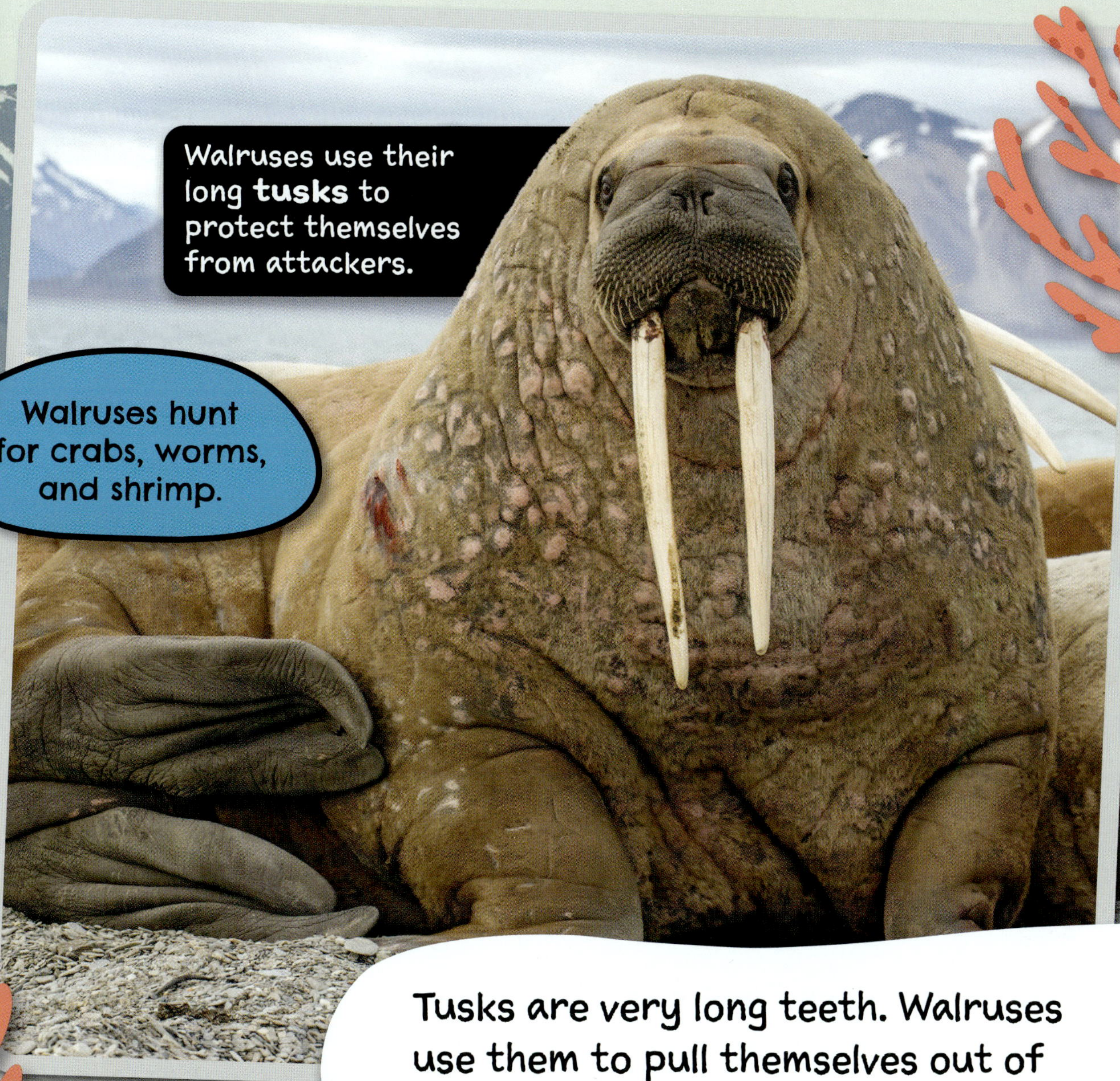

Walruses use their long **tusks** to protect themselves from attackers.

Walruses hunt for crabs, worms, and shrimp.

Tusks are very long teeth. Walruses use them to pull themselves out of the water onto ice sheets.

GALAPAGOS SEA LION

Galapagos sea lions live on the beaches of the Galapagos Islands.

Galapagos sea lions hunt in shallow waters and eat fish. Sometimes they eat squid and octopuses.

These sea lions don't swim too far from shore because it puts them in danger. In deeper waters, they might be eaten by sharks and orcas.

Baby sea lions stay close to their mothers until they are about a year old.

ORCA

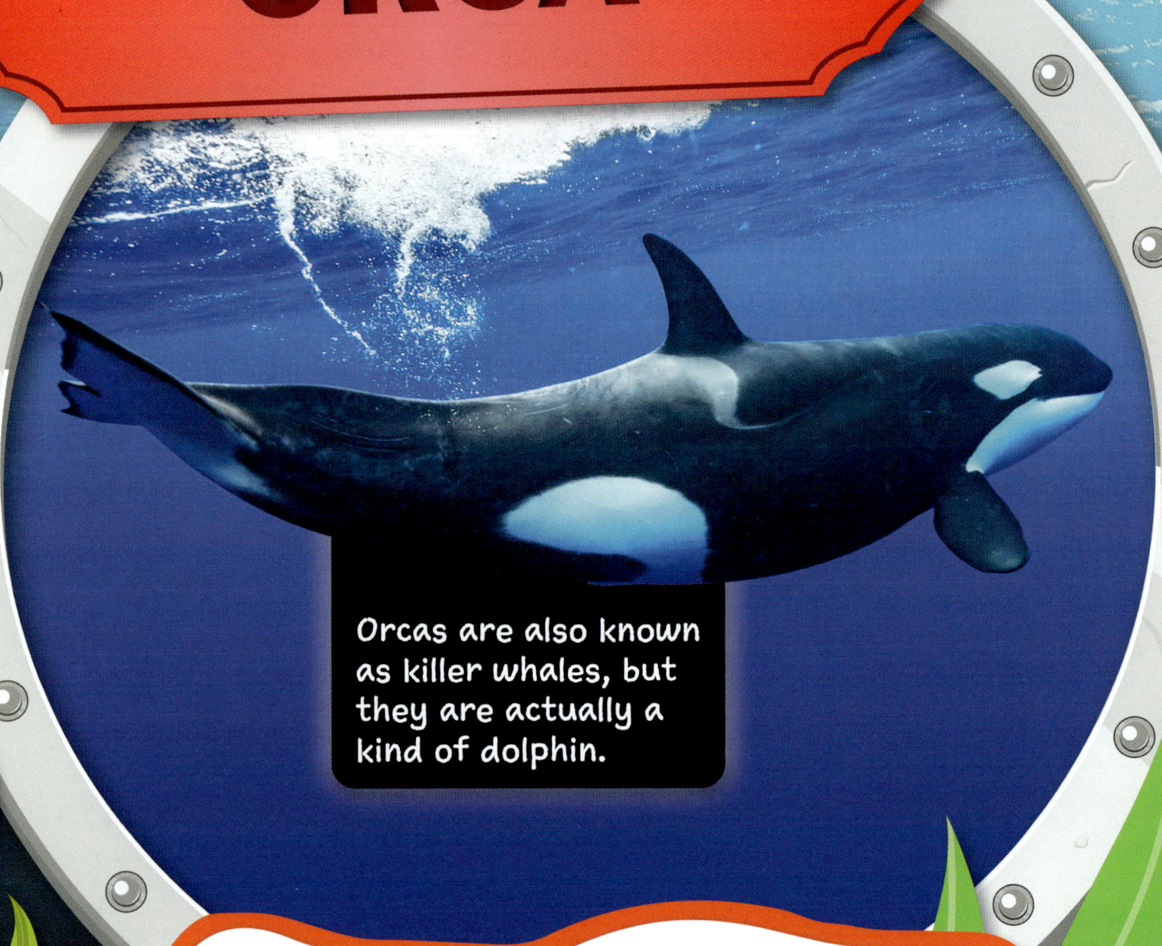

Orcas are also known as killer whales, but they are actually a kind of dolphin.

Orcas are the largest member of the dolphin family. They are very smart.

Orcas are powerful predators. They eat fish, seals, and even whales. Sometimes they hunt penguins, squid, and seabirds.

Orcas live and hunt in groups called pods.

ELEPHANT SEAL

Elephant seals get their name from the shape of the male seal's nose. It looks like an elephant's trunk.

Elephant seals are the biggest seals in the world.

Elephant seals are good divers. They can stay underwater for two hours at a time.

Elephant seals dive for meals of fish and squid.

RINGED SEAL

Ringed seals eat fish. They also eat shrimp.

Ringed seals are the smallest kind of seal. They are the most common type found in the Arctic.

These seals use the claws on their front flippers to carve through thick Arctic ice. This helps them make breathing holes.

Baby ringed seals are known as pups.

Ringed seals can dig holes through ice that is almost 7 feet (2 m) thick.

THANKS FOR VISITING!

Thank you for stopping by the aquarium. If you like marvelous mammals, there are things you can do to keep them safe.

Many animals are in danger of losing their **habitats**.

Rising air and water temperatures are harming sea habitats.

Using **fuel** for energy is making the air and water warmer. But there are some things you can do at home to help.

- Turn off lights when you leave a room.
- Try to walk or ride a bike instead of using a car.
- Wear more layers instead of turning the heat up.

GLOSSARY

fuel something that is burned to make heat or energy

habitats the places in nature where plants and animals live

mermaids animals that are part human and part fish

pods groups of whales or dolphins that live together

predators animals that hunt other animals for food

prey animals that are hunted by other animals for food

shallow not deep

tusks long, pointed teeth such as those on an elephant or a walrus

INDEX